MELBA LISTON
Trombone

DOT SAUTER
Bass

LIL HARDIN
Piano

T0003073

For my mama
—A.S.

MAKE ME A WORLD is an imprint dedicated to exploring the vast possibilities of contemporary childhood.
We strive to imagine a universe in which no young person is invisible, in which no kid's story is erased, in which
no glass ceiling presses down on the dreams of a child. Then we publish books for that world, where kids ask hard
questions and we struggle with them together, where dreams stretch from eons ago into the future and we do
our best to provide road maps to where these young folks want to be. We make books where the children
of today can see themselves and each other. When presented with fences, with borders, with limits,
with all the kinds of chains that hobble imaginations and hearts, we proudly say—no.

Mama Mable's All-Gal Big Band

JAZZ EXTRAVAGANZA!

Written and illustrated by

Annie Sieg

MAKE ME A WORLD

New York

All the men had gone to war.

Most women had to stay
to take care of our lives back home
while the soldiers were away.

We cooked and cleaned
(grown-ups and kids!).

We welded,
sawed, and sewed.

We sealed our letters with a kiss

and signed
them X and O.

We missed our fathers, brothers, friends—
but sisterhood was dear.
And then one day the news proclaimed:

**"Mama Mable's
band is here!"**

In times of war, it's hard to find
a cause for celebration.
So Mama Mable formed her band
to cheer up this good nation.

She gathered girls from near and far—

the bold,
the bright,
the brilliant.

To say with music what we felt,
our fears, hopes, and resilience.

A drummer warmed up
on her snare—

rat-a-tat-tatting
a big band boom!

A pianist played
the black-and-whites,

**fingers flying
through the tunes.**

There was a stunning trumpeter,
who clearly loved the show.

She'd tap her feet

and puff her cheeks

A long-haired girl played saxophone
with passion and with flair.
She took a slow, deep breath, and then

her sweet notes
filled the air.

Another girl embraced the bass,
her fingers

thrum-
bum-
bumming.

And we could not believe our ears
when the slide trombone went humming.

Finally she took the stage,
the leader of the band,

Mama Mable crooned and said,

"Let's give these gals a hand!"

When the show came to a close,
we begged them all to stay.
We'd had the most fantastic time.
They couldn't go away!

As they turned to say goodbye,
my face began to fall.
"Don't be sad," Mama Mable said.
"We're sisters, after all."

And with those parting words,
the band loaded up their things:
the slide trombone, the heavy bass,
the saxophone and strings.

Off they went to another town
to sing and dance and play.

And as for us, we'd never forget
the music from that day.

Music—it can mend the soul
when times call for some healing.

So find the music in *your* town.
Go out and share this feeling!

MAKE ME A WORLD

I am a big fan of the present. Sure, we have plenty of problems today, things that worry or concern me . . . but yesterday? The past always seems to hold worlds that would have limited me and the folks I love.

Once in a blue moon, however, there is an episode in history that I hope will point the way to the future. Such is the case with the subject of the book you have in your hands. In the 1940s during World War II, when women in the United States took over many jobs that had previously been held by men, a group of women took their places at the forefront of jazz.

Jazz was already a music form bristling with possibility, diversity, and openness. There had been women involved from its beginnings, but the doors of opportunity that swung wide due to the circumstances of war allowed female musicians to create a unique place for themselves.

Annie Sieg's *Mama Mable* is an invitation to this place—a riot of music and color, a community of sound and participation, a slice of the past—that has much less to do with yesterday than today.

I am still a big fan of the present, but if I could just once go to hear Mama Mable's All-Gal Big Band Extravaganza, I might just take a ticket to this past—the kind of yesterday that I hope looks like tomorrow.

Christopher Myers

◆ A Note from the Author ◆

I have a hard time pinpointing any one woman who inspired *Mama Mable's All-Gal Big Band Jazz Extravaganza!* The big band era marked a time when women from all walks of life came together and, for the first time, were able to pursue careers as professional touring musicians. Icons like Billie Holiday, Carmen McRae, Nina Simone, and Ella Fitzgerald revolutionized music with their vocal talents, and the character of Mama Mable is a salute to them all. While the band depicted in this story is fictional, the women were inspired by real historical figures, among them Viola Smith, Lil Hardin, Valaida Snow, Willie Mae Wong, Dot Sauter, and Melba Liston—each with a fascinating story of her own.

As a dance teacher, I have had many opportunities to observe the way music changes people. Good music can help heal heartache. It can form communities, bring out people's bravery or vulnerability, and tell their stories. In my personal experience, swing is the ultimate expression of this power. Born out of an era of oppression and uncertainty, big band swing is a wild and joyous rebellion. No matter what mood I'm in, listening to swing music lifts me up. It makes me want to laugh and smile and move my body. I am honored to have a chance to tell a story about an art form that means so much to me, and to represent some of the brilliant women who helped define the genre.

—Annie Sieg

VALAIDA SNOW
Trumpet

WILLIE MAE WONG
Saxophone

VIOLA SMITH
Drums